Elephant Jokes
100+ Funny Elephant Jokes

Johnny B. Laughing

DEDICATION

This book is dedicated to everyone that loves a funny joke.
Laughter is one of the best gifts you can give. It always puts a smile
on your face, warms your heart, and makes you feel great.

CONTENTS

FUNNY ELEPHANT JOKES

Q: What happened when the elephant sat on the car?

A: Everyone knows a Mercedes bends!

Q: What happened when two elephants jumped off a cliff?

A: BOOM BOOM!

Q: Why do elephants do well in school?

A: Because they have a lot of grey matter!

Q: What do you call an elephant that can't do math?

A: Dumbo!

Q: How do you know that peanuts are fattening?

A: Have you ever seen a skinny elephant?

Q: When should you feed milk to a baby elephant?

A: When it's a baby elephant!

Q: Why did the elephant eat the candle?

A: For light refreshment!

Q: Have you heard about the elephant that went on a crash diet?

A: He wrecked three cars, a bus, and two fire engines!

Q: Why do elephants eat raw food?

A: Because they don't know how to cook!

Q: Why are elephants wiser than chickens?

A: Have you ever heard of Kentucky Fried Elephant?!

Q: How can you tell if there is an elephant in your dessert?

A: You get very lumpy ice cream!

Q: What did the grape say when the elephant stood on it?

A: Nothing, it just let out a little wine!

Q: How do you get an elephant into a matchbox?

A: Take all the matches out first!

Q: What did the hotel manager say to the elephant that couldn't pay his bill?

A: Pack your trunk and clear out!

Q: Why did the elephant cross the road?

A: Because the chicken was having a day off!

Q: How does an elephant get out of a small car?

A: The same way that he got in!

Q: How do you fit five elephants into a car?

A: Two in the front, two in the back and the other in the glove compartment!

Q: Why do elephants have trunks?

A: Because they would look silly carrying suitcases!

Q: What kind of elephant lives in Antarctica?

A: Cold ones!

Q: What pill would you give to an elephant that can't sleep?

A: Trunkquilizers!

Q: What's the difference between an elephant and a gooseberry?

A: A gooseberry is green!

Q: What's the difference between an African elephant and an Indian elephant?

A: About 3,000 miles!

Q: Why are elephants grey?

A: So you can tell them apart from flamingos!

Q: What's the difference between an elephant and a banana?

A: Have you ever tried to peel an elephant?

Q: What's the difference between a sick elephant and seven days?

A: One is a weak one and the other one week!

Q: What's the difference between an elephant and a piece of paper?

A: You can't make a paper airplane out of an elephant!

Q: How do you tell the difference between an elephant and a mouse?

A: Try picking them up!

Q: What's the difference between an elephant and a bad pupil?

A: One rarely bites and the other barely writes!

Q: What's the difference between an injured elephant and bad weather?

A: One roars with pain and the other pours with rain!

Q: What's grey, beautiful and wears glass slippers?

A: Cinderelephant!

Q: What's grey, has a wand, huge wings, and gives money to elephants?

A: The tusk fairy!

Q: What's grey, carries a bunch of flowers and cheers you up when you're ill?

A: A get wellephant!

Q: What's grey but turns red?

A: An embarrassed elephant!

Q: What's grey and lights up?

A: An electric elephant!

Q: What's as big as an elephant but weighs nothing?

A: An elephant's shadow!

Q: What has 3 tails, 4 trunks and 6 feet?

A: An elephant with spare parts!

Q: What goes up slowly and comes down quickly?

A: An elephant in a lift!

Q: What's grey and wrinkly and jumps every twenty seconds?

A: An elephant with hiccups!

Q: What's blue and has big ears?

A: An elephant at the North Pole!

Q: What weighs 4 tons and is bright red?

A: An elephant holding its breath!

Q: What's big, grey and flies straight up?

A: An elecopter!

Q: What's big and grey and protects you from the rain?

A: An umbrellaphant!

Q: What's yellow on the outside and grey on the inside?

A: An elephant disguised as a banana!

Q: What's big and grey and lives in a lake in Scotland?

A: The Loch Ness Elephant!

Q: What's grey and goes round and round?

A: An elephant in a washing machine!

Q: What's grey and never needs ironing?

A: A drip dry elephant!

Q: What's grey, stands in a river when it rains, and doesn't get wet?

A: An elephant with an umbrella!

Q: What's big and grey and wears a mask?

A: The elephantom of the opera!

Q: What's grey and moves at a hundred miles an hour?

A: A jet-propelled elephant!

Q: Why does an elephant wear sneakers?

A: So that he can sneak up on mice!

Q: Why were the elephants thrown out of the swimming pool?

A: Because they couldn't hold their trunks up!

Q: Why did the elephant paint himself with different colors?

A: Because he wanted to hide in the coloring box!

Q: How does an elephant get down from a tree?

A: He sits on a leaf and waits until autumn!

Q: How do you hire an elephant?

A: Stand it on four bricks!

Q: Who do elephants get their Christmas presents from?

A: Elephanta Claus!

Q: What do elephants sing at Christmas?

A: Noel-ephants, Noel-ephants!

Q: What do you get if you cross a parrot with an elephant?

A: An animal that tells you everything that it remembers!

Q: What did the elephant say when the man grabbed him by the tail?

A: This is the end of me!

Q: What is a baby elephant after he is five weeks old?

A: Six weeks old!

Q: Why did the elephant jump in the lake when it began to rain?

A: To stop getting wet!

Q: What did the elephant say to the famous detective?

A: It's ele-mentary, my dear Sherlock!

Q: What do elephants say as a compliment?

A: You look elephantastic!

Q: What is an elephant's favorite film?

A: Elephantasia!

Q: Who lost a herd of elephants?

A: Big Bo Peep!

Q: What do elephants do in the evenings?

A: Watch elevision!

Q: What do you do with old cannon balls?

A: Give them to elephants to use as marbles!

Q: What is stronger, an elephant or a snail?

A: A snail because it carries its house, an elephant just carries its trunk!

Q: What do you find in an elephant's graveyard?

A: Elephantoms!

Q: What animals were last to leave the ark?

A: The elephants because they had to pack their trunks!

Q: Why do elephants have trunks?

A: Because they have no pockets to put things in!

Q: What do you give an elephant with big feet?

A: Plenty of room!

Q: How to elephants talk to each other?

A: By elephone!

Q: What do you call the rabbit up the elephant's sweater?

A: Terrified!

Q: What do you call an elephant creeping through the jungle in the middle of the night?

A: Russell!

Q: What do you call an elephant that lays across the middle of a tennis court?

A: Annette!

Q: What do you call an elephant with a carrot in each ear?

A: Anything you want because he can't hear you!

Q: Why don't elephants like playing cards in the jungle?

A: Because of all the cheetahs!

Q: What's the best way to see a charging herd of elephants?

A: On television!

Q: What did Tarzan say when he saw the elephants coming?

A: Here come the elephants!

Q: What is an easy way to get a wild elephant?

A: Get a tame one and annoy it!

Q: Why do elephants jump across rivers?

A: So they won't step on the fish.

Q: Why do elephants squirt water through their noses?

A: If they squirted it through their tails, it'd be very difficult to aim.

Q: Why do elephants live in the jungle?

A: Because it's out of the high rent district.

Q: Why don't elephants like martinis?

A: Have you ever tried to get an olive out of your nose?

Q: Why are elephants large, grey and wrinkly?

A: Because if they were small, round and white, they would be aspirins.

Q: Why do elephants prefer peanuts to caviar?

A: Because they're easier to get at the ballpark.

Q: Why did the gum cross the road?

A: Because it was under the elephant's foot.

Q: What does a bald elephant wear for a toupee?

A: A sheep.

Q: What do you get if you cross an elephant with the abominable snowman?

A: A jumbo yeti.

Q: How does an elephant go up a tree?

A: It stands on an acorn and waits for it to grow.

Q: How do you make an elephant sandwich?

A: First of all, you get a very large loaf of bread.

Q: How do you raise a baby elephant?

A: With a fork lift truck!

Q: What is worse than raining cats and dogs?

A: Raining elephants!

Q: Why is an elephant braver than a hen?

A: Because the elephant isn't chicken!

Q: Why do elephants have short tails?

A: Because they can't remember long stories!

Q: What did the baby elephant get when the daddy elephant sneezed?

A: Out of the way!

Q: How do you stop an angry elephant from charging?

A: Take away its credit cards.

MAZE #1

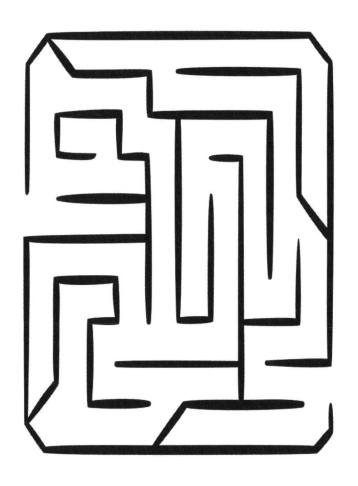

MAZE #2

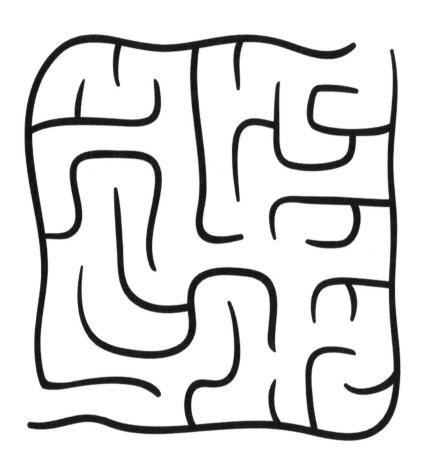

MAZE #3

MAZE #4

MAZE #5

MAZE #6

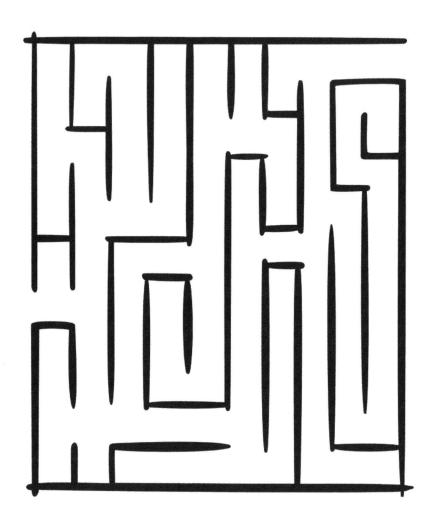

MAZE #7

MAZE #8

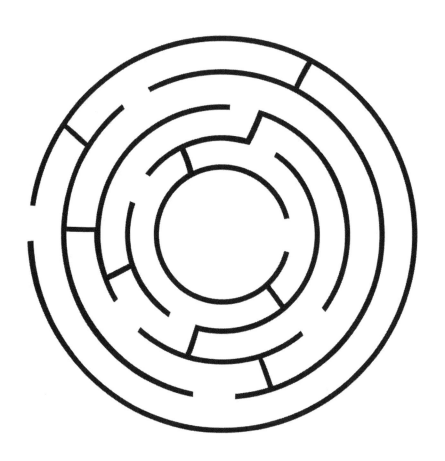

MAZE SOLUTIONS 1-4

MAZE SOLUTIONS 5-8

ABOUT THE AUTHOR

The Joke King, Johnny B. Laughing is a best-selling children's joke book author. He is a jokester at heart and enjoys a good laugh, pulling pranks on his friends, and telling funny and hilarious jokes!

For more funny joke books just search for
JOHNNY B. LAUGHING on Amazon

-or-

Visit the website:
www.funny-jokes-online.weebly.com

Made in the USA
Las Vegas, NV
26 September 2021